The Sorcerer's Scrapbook

or "Why I am a Wizard"

Being

The Life and Times of Nicodemus Magnus,
Doctor of Magic and Sorcerer to the Duke

TOLD IN HIS OWN WORDS

Michael Berenstain

RANDOM HOUSE 🏠 NEW YORK

For Odile

Library of Congress Cataloging in Publication Data:
Berenstain, Michael. The sorcerer's scrapbook, or, "Why I am a wizard."
SUMMARY: A wizard tries to help a duke defy fate by locating a unicorn.
[1. Unicorns—Fiction. 2. Magic—Fiction] I. Title. PZ7. B44827So [Fic] 80-5754
ISBN: 0-394-84731-8 (trade); 0-394-94731-2 (lib. bdg.) AACR2

Manufactured in the United States of America
1 2 3 4 5 6 7 8 9 0

Being a sorcerer isn't easy.
Many a sleepless night I've spent
poring over dusty old books, searching
for a half-forgotten spell.

And the foul potions and stinks I have brewed! I choke just to think of them.

The weary days I've spent casting horoscopes.

The evil spirits I've dealt with! There must have been a million.

And the old bones I've
dug up—what a dismal job!

But I must admit that sorcery has
its good points, too.
There's the quaint old tradition of
changing lead into gold.

And the simple joy of a
neatly cast spell.

Not to mention that
fine, proud feeling of
being respected and
admired by all.

Wealth and fame are fine, indeed,
but more important to the true sorcerer
is the thrill of exploring the Unknown.

How, you may ask, did I become a sorcerer? The answer goes back to my student days.

My teacher was Albertus the Wise—"Old Bert" we called him—greatest sorcerer of his day.

I learned a great deal from him before he threw me out.

ME

After that I became a
wandering magician—traveling
here and there, amazing the
mob—until one day I came to
the little town of Dunkledorf.

My talents soon came to the
notice of the local Duke, Wilhelm
the Grand, who begged me to
become his Court Sorcerer.

One of my first duties was to cast the Duke's horoscope.

A horoscope, I should explain, is a map of the stars at the time of a person's birth. By studying it, we can predict that person's future.

The horoscope I drew for the Duke was ruled by Mars—Sign of War and Anger—and by Saturn—Sign of Misfortune. Together, they pointed to danger from Wrath and Pride.

But, more alarming, the position of Scorpio—Sign of Death—told me that the Duke was fated to die of poison. And quite soon!

The Duke was somewhat upset by this news.

"It's an outrage!" he roared. "You are plotting with my enemies to poison my food and drink!"

"But, my Lord," I protested. "Your horoscope is not my fault . . . the stars never lie."

"Then you're fired!" bellowed the Duke.

I thought quickly.

"Of course," I remarked, "there may be a way out."

"Oh? And what might that be?" asked the Duke.

"Unicorn horn," I replied.

"Unicorn horn?"

Saevus et Audax

"Yes, my Lord—the horn of the unicorn is proof against all poison. If poisoned wine is poured into a goblet made of this magical horn, the wine becomes pure and wholesome."

"Well, then," said the Duke, "get me a unicorn."

"But, my Lord!" I gasped. "The unicorn is the rarest, the fiercest, and the fleetest of all creatures! How am I to capture one?"

"That's your problem!" he snapped, and abruptly dismissed me.

I returned to my study to begin to learn about the unicorn.

The unicorn is a marvelous beast. It has the
head, neck, and body of a horse, but the legs,
feet, and tail of a goat. It has a goat's beard, too.
Its horn, however, is unlike any other creature's.

One touch of a unicorn's horn
will purify an entire lake, such
is its virtue.

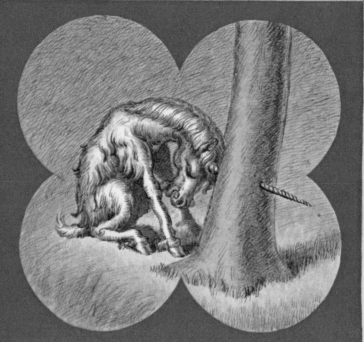

In its wrath, the unicorn has
been known to run trees through
with its horn. Held fast, it may
perish for want of food.

The unicorn lives to a great
age, some say a thousand, some
two thousand years.

No hunter can catch the
unicorn, such is its swiftness.

Only the Wildmen of the
Forest have ridden them. The
Wildmen drop from the trees
onto the unsuspecting unicorns
and ride them for sport.

It is further said that only
a fair maiden who is pure of
heart can capture a unicorn.
She has but to play a lute in
the depths of the forest and
the unicorn, tamed and trusting,
will come and lay its head upon
her lap.

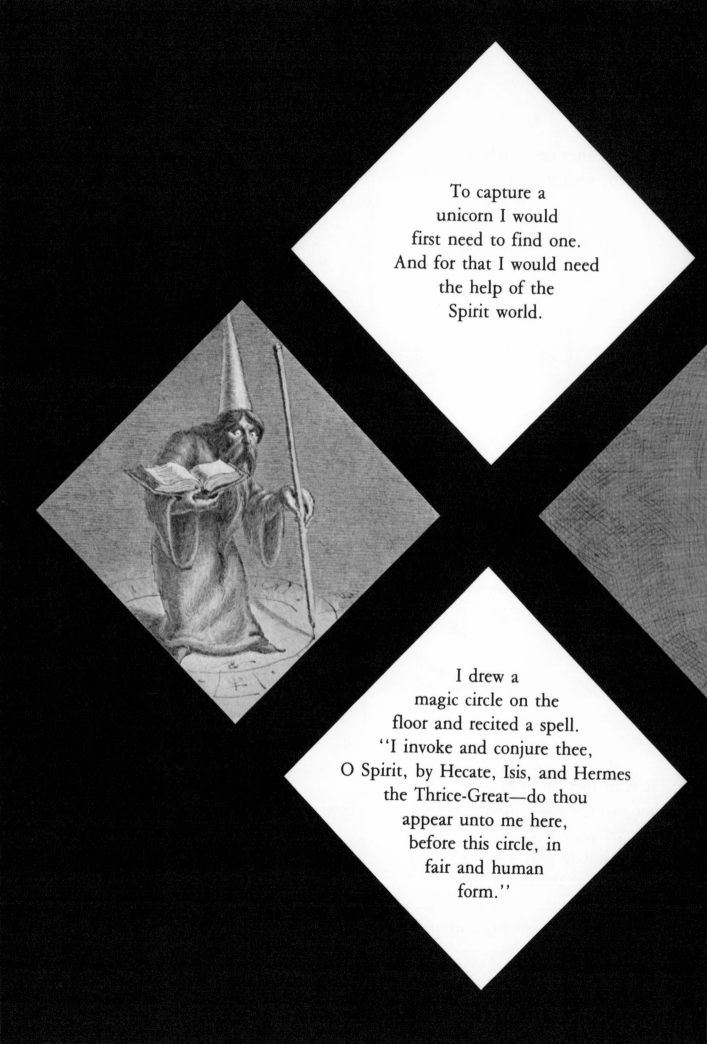

To capture a
unicorn I would
first need to find one.
And for that I would need
the help of the
Spirit world.

I drew a
magic circle on the
floor and recited a spell.
"I invoke and conjure thee,
O Spirit, by Hecate, Isis, and Hermes
the Thrice-Great—do thou
appear unto me here,
before this circle, in
fair and human
form."

It worked!

"What would'st thou?" the Spirit asked.

"Tell me, O Fair Spirit," I said. "Do you know where I might find a unicorn?"

She sighed deeply.

"'Tis many an age since I have seen a unicorn," she said. "But I know of many strange places where strange creatures dwell."

And so we set off into the Wilds.

We traveled until we came to high mountains.
There we found a narrow ravine and, in the
ravine, a dark cave.

"Do unicorns live here?" I asked.

"Unicorns?" cried a voice, and a large,
ugly head appeared from the cave. It was
a dragon!

"You mean those things with the horn?"
it asked. "Now let me see . . . no, I
don't believe I know one. But then, what
do *I* know? I'm just a dragon! I have
troubles of my own. Why, just the other
day . . ."

And the dragon began a strange tale.

was walking along, minding my own business, when I met a young lady.

'' 'How do you do?' said I. 'Nice day?'

'' 'EEEK!' she screamed, 'A DRAGON!'
'' 'Madam!' I exclaimed. 'Calm yourself!'
'' 'EEEK!' she screamed again.

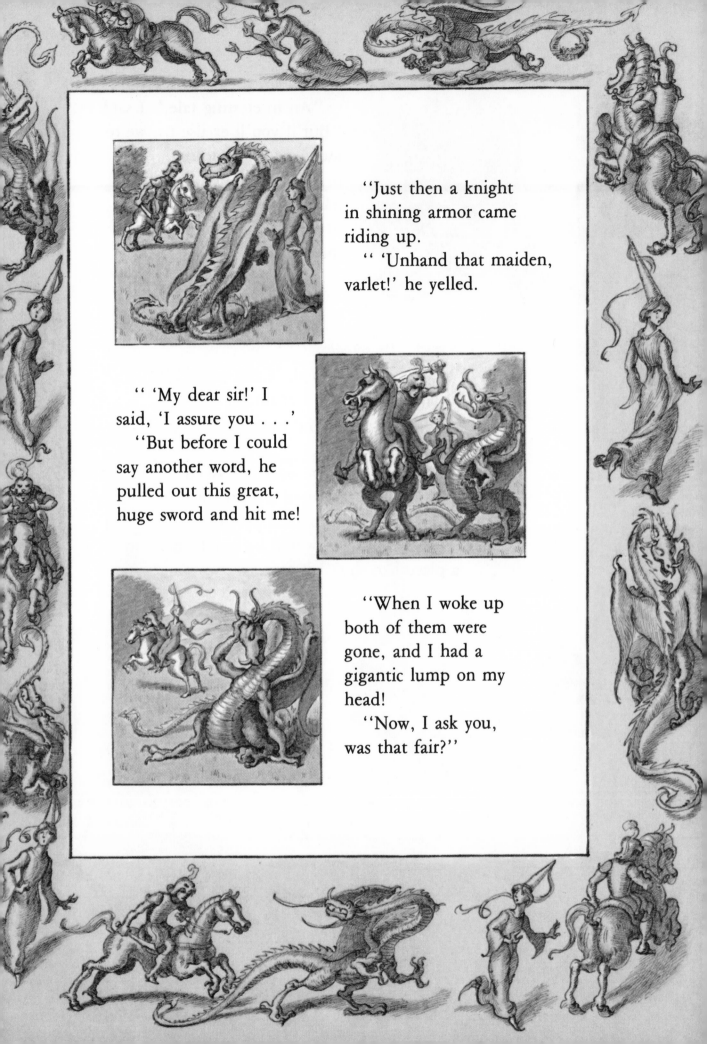

"Just then a knight in shining armor came riding up.

" 'Unhand that maiden, varlet!' he yelled.

" 'My dear sir!' I said, 'I assure you . . .'

"But before I could say another word, he pulled out this great, huge sword and hit me!

"When I woke up both of them were gone, and I had a gigantic lump on my head!

"Now, I ask you, was that fair?"

"An interesting tale," I said. "But if you'll excuse us, we're looking for a unicorn."

"Well!" huffed the dragon. "Don't mind me! *I'm* just a dragon!" And he disappeared into the cave.

We pressed on and came to a dark and dreary swamp.

"Do unicorns live *here*?" I asked.

"Unicorns!" snorted a deep voice.

A huge griffin loomed over us.

"What unicorn would be caught dead in a place like this?" it growled.

We left the swamp and came to a wide plain. Suddenly
a huge bird came flapping up. It was a phoenix!

"Hurry! Hurry!" it cried. "See me burst into flames
and rise from the ashes! Only happens once every thousand
years! Don't miss it! Tickets just sixpence!"

"No, thank you," I said.

"Cheapskates!" it muttered and flew off.

Soon we came to a deep
forest. All was dark and
still. The only sound was
the whispering of the
leaves.

And then something
moved among the trees.

It was a unicorn!

At once I set about casting a spell over the elusive creature.

But spells are tricky things, and I must have made a mistake or two, for the results were not quite what I'd had in mind.

Undaunted, I brewed a magic potion with newts' eyes, bats' wings, mandrake roots—the usual—and set it out for the unicorn.

It didn't work.

There must have been something missing.

Gold dust, perhaps?

Gold dust is hard to find and harder, still, to make. My own (secret) method is as follows:

How to Make Gold

Take 3 ounces lead, 1 ounce alum,
2 ounces saltpeter, and 6 ounces quicksilver.
Melt them all down in a large pot.

Note: Because of the poisonous fumes
given off during this process, it is wise to
eat bread thickly spread with butter to
lessen the effect.

Place the mixture in a distilling
furnace for 8 hours, or until the
receiving vessel is full of a pale
yellow liquid.

Distill the liquid in a pelican
flask for 12 more hours.
It should turn bright orange.

Pour the orange liquid into several alembic bottles, and place the bottles in a water bath. Heat slowly for 6 days. At the end of this time the liquid should have turned a deep red.

This is called Lion's Blood.

Place the Lion's Blood in a retort and boil until only a black residue remains.

This is called Dragon's Venom.

Pour the Dragon's Venom into an egg flask full of alcohol. Fine gold flakes should appear at the bottom.

If they do not, you have done something wrong and should start over.

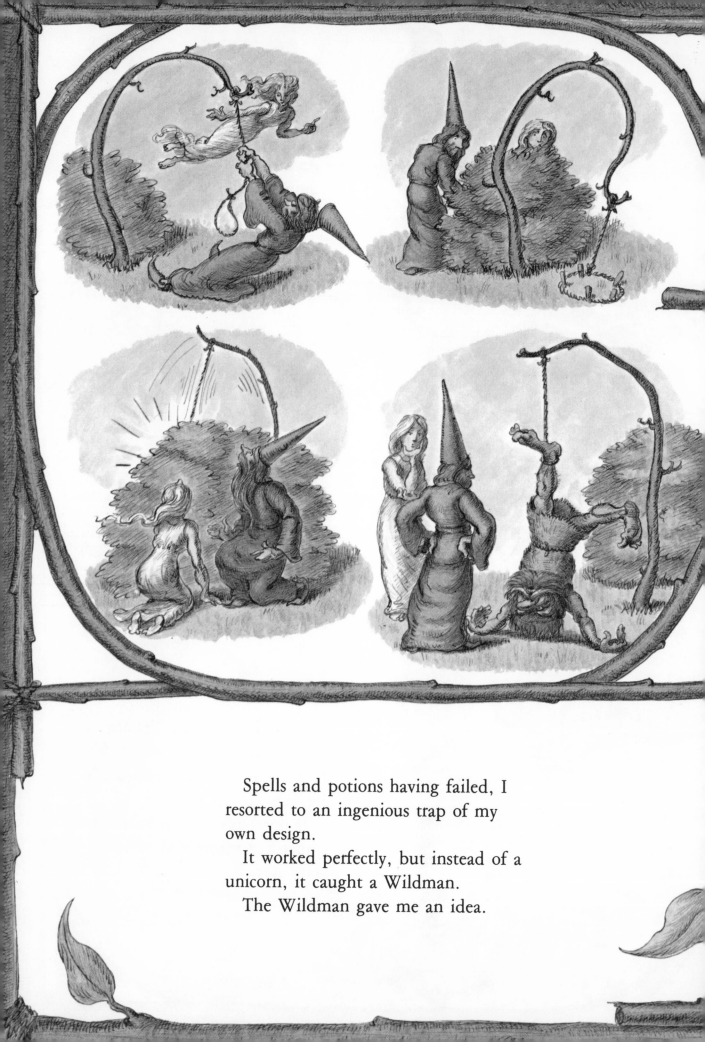

Spells and potions having failed, I resorted to an ingenious trap of my own design.

It worked perfectly, but instead of a unicorn, it caught a Wildman.

The Wildman gave me an idea.

I knew that Wildmen of the Forest captured
unicorns by dropping upon them from trees.
Perhaps my Wildman could do the same?
He was, unfortunately, a bit out of practice.

Downcast by this final failure, I was about to
return and admit defeat to the Duke when the
Spirit exclaimed, "Hark! Someone comes!"

And there, sure enough, was a young woman
making her way through the trees.

To my surprise, I recognized her. It was Duke
Wilhelm's daughter, Wilhelmina!

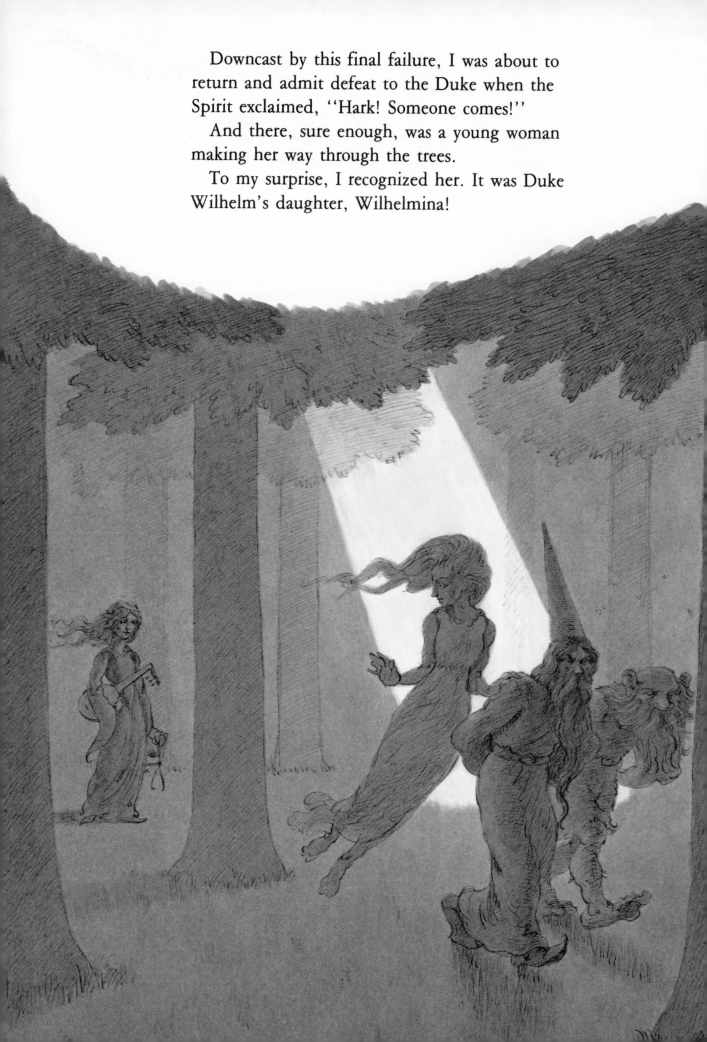

She carried a lute and, as we watched unseen, she sat in a clearing and began to play.

The music was sweet and pure. It blended with the whispering leaves and the songs of the birds.

Then, moving among the shadows, the unicorn appeared.

It sat beside the maiden and laid its head upon her lap.

I was astounded. But the Spirit just smiled. "Only a fair maiden who is pure of heart . . ." she began.

"Yes, yes, I know," I snapped. "We must inform the Duke at once!"

We rushed to the Duke and whispered
our news to him.

The Duke was pleased.

"Good!" he cried. "We shall have a
Unicorn Hunt!"

And so all the Duke's huntsmen and
grooms and horses and dogs were made
ready for the Great Unicorn Hunt.

The hunt galloped into the deep forest. Silently the hunters approached the clearing and set up their nets.

Then they charged. The unicorn fled straight into the nets and was held fast. Spearmen ran up for the kill.

But the Duke's daughter begged her father to spare the unicorn.

Shamed, he called off his men.

Roped and bound, the unicorn
was carried back, alive, to the castle.

There it was caged in the
Duke's menagerie, and all
came to admire the beautiful
creature.

The Duke had promised his
daughter that the unicorn would
not be harmed. But I did not
trust him.

That night I decided to keep watch over the unicorn's cage. My friends and I crept silently into the dark courtyard.

No sooner had we hidden than who should appear but the Duke himself!

He drew his sword and approached the unicorn's cage.

But the cage was empty!

"What's this?" he gasped. "My enemies have stolen the unicorn!"

Then he saw his daughter hiding in the shadows.

"So!" he roared, seizing her. "It was you! You value a dumb animal more than your own father."

"No!" she cried. "It isn't true!"

She reached into her cloak and brought out . . . the unicorn's horn!

"I released the unicorn," she admitted,
"but only after I had found this in the cage!"
"But," I gasped, astonished. "How can
that be!"

Suddenly the Wildman began to jump
up and down.
"I know! I know!" he cried gleefully.
"Horn fall off! Yes! Yes! Horn fall off!"

And so it had.

Just as deer shed their antlers every year, so, too, the unicorn sheds its horn every thousand years.

(I might point out that it was I, Nicodemus Magnus, who first brought this little-known fact to the attention of the Learned World.)

At last the Duke had his goblet made of unicorn horn and could drink his wine without fear of poisoning.

He ordered a great feast in celebration.

"A toast!" cried the Duke, raising his magic goblet. "To me! Duke Wilhelm the Grand! Foiler of the Fates and Mocker of the Heavens!"

"To the Duke!" everyone cried and raised their glasses.

At that moment there was a "whizzz!" and a "crack!" and an arrow knocked the goblet from the Duke's hand!

"Treason!" he cried.

"Treason!" everyone cried. "Find the traitor!"

The palace was searched from top to bottom, but no one was found.

The Duke's hand had been scratched by the arrow, but he made light of the wound and the feast went on.

That night the Duke's hand began to throb. He fell ill and, in spite of all I did, he died in the morning.

It was not the wine that had been poisoned—but the arrow!

I have since grown old and my hair has turned white. I have learned much and forgotten much.

But one thing I will always remember . . .

The stars never lie.